DISCARD

THE GOOD MESSAGE
OF HANDSOME LAKE

UNICORN KEEPSAKE SERIES

JOSEPH BRUCHAC

The Good Message of
HANDSOME LAKE

GREENSBORO: Unicorn Press, Inc.

Copyright © 1979 Joseph Bruchac
Original woodblock by Rita Corbin

Three of the thirty-four poems in this collection have been previously published in magazines: "Midwinter at Onondaga" in *The South Dakota Review*, "Tonawanda" in *The Spirit That Moves Us*, and "Thanksgiving Prayer" in *River Styx*. The editors of those magazines are gratefully acknowledged.

Library of Congress Number 77-973335
I.S.B. Number (cloth) 0-87775-112-9
I.S.B. Number (paper) 0-87775-113-7

Unicorn Press, Inc.
Post Office Box 3307
Greensboro, North Carolina 27402

CONTENTS

PRAYER

Each gathering of The Longhouse People begins with a Thanksgiving Speech, words which express greeting and thanks and happiness for the existence of all that is good around them. Let us begin, then, by putting our minds together to give thanks. Let us give thanks with care and with love for:

The People
The Plants
The Water
The Trees
The Animals
The Birds
The Three Sisters (Corn, Squash and Beans)
The Wind
The Thunderers
The Sun
The Moon
The Stars
The Four Messengers
Our Creator

Give it your thought that we may do it properly and our minds will continue to be so.

INTRODUCTION

The poems and translations in this book draw from a number of sources. One of the most important of these is Arthur Parker's *The Code of Handsome Lake, The Seneca Prophet*. Equally important has been my contact with contemporary Iroquois people, people who have managed to preserve their distinct cultural identity as The People of the Longhouse, even after centuries of attempted cultural genocide. I am grateful for the things I have learned from such teachers as Ray Fadden and Alice Papineau. I also know that I have not learned a great deal. Any mistakes in this book are my own and I only hope that my teachers, both present and future, will continue to help me in my attempts to walk in balance and say things as they should be said.

Handsome Lake was a great prophet. He took noble elements already present in his culture and offered them again to his people in the form of a fresh vision. It was a revitalization greatly needed at a time when the Iroquois had been demoralized by betrayal and bad treaties after the American Revolution. Anthony Wallace's *The Death and Rebirth of the Seneca Nation* tells the story of those years better than any other history yet written on the subject.

Handsome Lake, however, did not "found" Iroquois religion. I stress this because, as Kakwirakeron, a traditional Mohawk, said to me, "If you speak of Handsome Lake as being the founder of Iroquois religion in 1800, people will think we had no religion at all before that." Kakwirakeron's words do not express pessimism, but, I am afraid, a very clear grasp of the patronizing attitude most people in the Western World take towards Indian people — even as they envy and admire them as "noble savages."

Perhaps Handsome Lake can be compared to John Wesley, although that comparison would hold more water if Wesley were a former soldier and leader of his people who were surrounded by a larger nation out to exterminate them at the time of his evangelism. A better comparison might be with Wovoka, the Paiute religious leader whose visions of a new way led to the Ghost Dance almost a century later — although Handsome Lake's great vision did not end, as did Wovoka's, in the bloody snow of a Wounded Knee. It continues today.

Whatever Handsome Lake's role, there can be no doubt that he was a man of intelligence and kindness. He was touched by a vision and he devoted his life to fulfilling it. His vision holds up many of the enlightened and humane teachings which were part of the life of his people long before the coming of the Europeans, teachings which have assisted his people to find their way back to the sacred circle, teachings which have a great deal to say not just to American Indian people, but to all human beings.

Freezing Moon 1977
Greenfield Center

THANKSGIVING

And now this is what Our Creator did.
Our Creator did indeed decide it
and it had to happen according to Our Creator's will.

There was one among us
who moved about on the Earth.
Illness took hold of him.
For a long time he lay helpless.
And, the way things were,
he had to be thankful
during the nights and days
and he thought
there must be Someone
who made all the things he was seeing.

And thereupon he repented everything,
all the things he thought he had done wrong
when he moved about on the Earth.
And indeed he was thankful
for each new thing that he saw.

And now it happened
that the Creator saw well
how the people on Earth were acting
It seemed that nowhere
was there any longer any guidance
for the minds of those who moved about.
And now it happened
that he sent The Four Messengers
to speak to our great one,
whom we used to call Ganio-dai'yo
when he moved about.

They gave him the responsibility
to tell us what would happen in the future.
And for a number of years
he told the words of the Creator.
And the way things went,
he labored until he collapsed.

Let there indeed be gratitude
that from time to time we now again
hear the words of the Creator.
And therefore let there be gratitude
that it is still continuing
as the Creator planned it.

Adapted from Wallace Chafe's translation
of part of a Thanksgiving Speech given
by Corbett Sundown.

I The Coming of the Good Message

I.

In the Strawberry Moon
Ganio-dai'yo woke
after two hours
in the Spirit World
to speak the first of his good words.

He had fought as a warrior
beside his brother, Cornplanter,
although he never boasted
of men that he had killed.

He had seen their lands
from Kinzua to Corydon
burning with Washington's wrath,
the good log houses of his Seneca people
and all their corn for the hungry season
gone into flames with Sullivan's passing,
the soil blackened, the fruit trees girdled.

The Quakers were moving
in those days
among the Keepers of the Western Door,
telling them to look within their hearts
to test what was truly good or bad.

There was much that was bad then
among his people, cheated of their land,
weakened with drink
and wondering when the Thunder rolled
if the Messengers
who once had freed
the people of the Longhouse from monsters
had forgotten them forever.

II.

In the Strawberry Moon
the message came
to Cornplanter
that his brother was dying.

When he went to him,
he found him lying
without breath
his spirit gone out
from his body,
though he had not died
for he came to himself again
and spoke:

I heard someone calling me
out of the house
and when I went
I found three men
holding bushes with berries
in their hands.

"Eat," they told me,
"We shall help you
and you shall live
to see such berries
grow ripe this summer.

The Creator is not pleased
to see your people drunk
and doing evil.
He knows not only
their deeds, Ganio-dai'yo,
but also their very thoughts."

III.

Then Ganio-dai'yo and Cornplanter
called the people into council
to tell them all that had been seen
and if they had dried berries enough
then all in the council would eat them.

It was done that day.

And all who were there
seemed deeply moved,
even Simmons, the Quaker missionary.

IV.

Then Ganio-dai'yo told Cornplanter
those three messengers had said to him
that they were four but the other person
had not yet come and would come to him soon.

For some weeks thereafter Ganio-dai'yo
remained in bad health
until he dreamed
the absent person came to him
and said he would take him along
if he wished to go
because he pitied him so much.

Ganio-dai'yo woke
and put on his best clothes,
calling for his brother
for he was afraid
he would not see him before he was gone.
Through the day Cornplanter stayed by Ganio-dai'yo
until, near evening, Ganio-dai'yo fainted
then recovered enough to say that he
would leave but only go so far
as to see his son and his brother's daughter
who had been dead that past year.

It was then his breath left him,
his limbs grew cold.
He went out of the world
to a place where a guide
dressed in a clear sky color appeared
carrying a single arrow and a bow.

V.

Ganio-dai'yo was taken
to his son and his niece.

Both were dressed in that color
of the clear sky.
Then he was told
of his one great fault —
the drinking of rum
and that it must cease
for those who drank
in such a manner
would never come
to that happy place.

And when he turned
to look toward the river
he saw many canoes
filled with kegs of whiskey
and one loading them
whose eyes were ugly,
the Maker of Evil
who often fooled
those who followed his way
into thinking him the Creator.

13

VI.

Then Ganio-dai'yo heard many things from his guide,
he was told that a great sickness
was about to come upon his people
unless they made their ways straight again.

When he went back they should join together
in worship at the White Dog Feast
to prevent that illness.

Then Ganio-dai'yo returned,
being told that he would see his guide
no more until the time arrived
for him to die — although if he
did not do right
he would not see him
even then.

VII.

Henry Simmons, the Quaker Missionary speaks:

On the day after the White Dog Feast
I found the old man much improved.
He spoke to me of many things.
He said some of our white ways were good
but that he liked some of the ways
of his own people very well.

Time would be needed to lead his people
from their set ways, but they would keep
such things which were good as the Worship dances,
their way of worshipping the Great Spirit.

It was then he remarked, astonishing me greatly,
that the white people had killed their own Saviour.

How he had heard of Him, I do not know
but could only reply it was the Jews
who killed Our Lord and neither did I
know but what the Indians were their descendents.

VIII.

For ten years Ganio-dai'yo taught
at Cornplanter's Town the way
which was given the name
Gai'wiio, the Good Message.

And when the Seneca went down
to Pittsburgh to trade their furs,
they returned with food and clothing,
not whiskey. Jars of sugar water
were now kept by the traders
to give the treat
which once had been of rum.

From Cornplanter's Town to Coldspring
was the first of four steps
Ganio-dai'yo would make.
From there he went to Cattaraugus
and his third step was to Tonawanda,
the place called Gajus'towanen,
"There where the Great Brightness is,"
where his wampum strings are kept.

In 1815 the vision came
after four years at Tonawanda.

The Four Messengers returned
to say he must go to Onondaga.
There he would sing his final song
where hands were stretched out,
pleading for him to come.

16

The old man, with a chosen few,
began the long walk to Onondaga.
Soon the number with him grew.
The prediction of his death was known.
It was clear where his steps were leading.

The first day they camped at Ganundasa'ga
and in the morning he told of the vision
of a woman who spoke to him.
Then they continued on their way.

The Four Messengers had told him, long ago,
that he must never be alone, but near Onondaga
he missed his favorite knife
and went back alone to find it.

When he returned, his strength was gone.
His followers helped him
go the last few miles
which took him to Onondaga.
There he spoke only of a plain pathway
which lay before him, a pathway
he followed a few days later.

Today a stone stands
near the Council House
at Onondaga.

It reads:

GA-NYAH-DI-YOH

AUTHOR OF THE PRESENT

INDIAN RELIGION

Born at

Cah-noh-wa-gus / Genesee Co., N.Y. 1735
Died Aug. 10, 1815
at Onondaga Reservation
HANDSOME LAKE

II Sections from the Gai'wiio
of Handsome Lake

CHILDREN

A woman punished
her children unjustly.
The Creator is sad
because of such things
and bids us tell you
they must cease.

Talk slowly and kindly
to children.
Never punish them unjustly.

If a child does not obey,
let the mother say,
"Come to the water
and I will dunk you."
And if the child
still does not obey
let her say this again.
If at the third time
obedience still has not come
then the child should be dunked
in the water.

But if the child cries for mercy
it must have it.

So they said and he said.
It was that way.

ADVICE FROM CHILDREN

Some parents do not listen
to the warnings of their children.

When a child says,
"Mother, you must stop wrongdoing,"
that child speaks straight words.

The Creator says that child speaks right
and the mother must obey.

Such words from any child are wonderful.
Any mother who regards them not
takes the wicked part.

The mother might answer,
"Daughter, stop your noise!
I know better than you,
you are only a child.
You can't change me by your words!"

Now when you take
this message to your people
tell them it is wrong
to speak that way to children.

So they said and he said.
It was that way.

POOR CHILDREN AND ORPHANS

When a woman hears hungry children
playing near her lodge,
she must call them in
and ask them to eat.

The Creator says that this is right,
for some children come of poor families
and have very little to eat.
Whoever feeds the poor and hungry
does right before the Creator.

When a woman sees an unfortunate girl
who has no parents and no settled home,
she must call her in and comb her hair
and help her mend her clothing

The Creator truly loves the poor.
When a woman does this,
she does right before the Creator.

We, the Four Messengers,
say that you must tell your people
to continue to do
such good things.

So they said and he said.
It was that way.

THE OLD

The Creator ordained
that people should live
to an old age.

When a woman becomes old
she will be without strength
and unable to work.

It is wrong to be unkind
to our Grandmothers.

The Creator forbids
unkindness to the Old.
We, the Four Messengers, say this.

The Creator made it
to be this way.
An old woman shall be
as a child again
and her grandchildren
shall care for her.
For only because she is,
they are.

So they said and he said.
It was that way.

FOOD

When a mother is ready
to feed her family
she sees someone coming
and hides the food
until the visitor is gone.

The Creator says
such ways are wicked.

The Creator made food
for all creatures
and it must be free for all.
He ordained that people
should live together.

Whenever a visitor enters a lodge
the woman must say,
"Sede'koni, Come eat,"
and the visitor
must always take
at least two or three bites
and say "Niaweh, Thank you."

Tell this to your people.

So they said and he said.
It was that way.

GOSSIP

It may happen that a woman
sets out to destroy good feelings
between her neighbors by telling stories.

She goes to a house and says,
"Because I love you
I will tell you a secret.
The woman in the next house
speaks evil about you!"

Thus one becomes angry
at her friend and speaks
hard words about her.

Then the one who carries gossip
goes to the other house and tells
those hard words to the former friend.

Then is the liar happy.
From house to house she hastens,
telling others of the feud she has started.

Human creatures should be kind
one to the other
and help each other
in the Creator's way.

When one woman visits another's house,
she must help with the work,
talk pleasantly
and if she relates jokes,
they must be on herself.

If she speaks harsh words,
the woman of the house must answer,
"I remember the desires of our Creator.
I cannot hear what you say."

Thus evil is cut off
at its beginning.

So they said and he said.
It was that way.

BOASTING

Now one man says
he is far more handsome
than all other men.
He boasts that he
is handsome and grand.
The Creator says
that this is wrong.
When a man is handsome
let him thank the Creator
for his good looks.

So they said.

Now another man says,
"I am strongest of all.
No one can throw me
to the ground!"
The Creator says
such boasting is evil.
The Creator gave
that man his strength
and therefore he
should thank the Giver.

So they said.

Now another man says,
"I am the swiftest
of all the runners in the world!"
He regards himself
as a mighty man and boasts before the people.
The Creator says
such boasting is evil.
The Creator gave
that man his speed.
That man should offer thanks,
not boast.

Now, we, the Four Messengers
say that your people
should stop their boasting.

So they said and he said.
It was that way.

FARMING

Three things done
by our younger brothers
are right to follow.

The white man works a tract of land
and harvests food for his family,
so if he should die
they have the ground for help.

If any of your people
have cultivated land
let them not be proud
on that account.

If one is proud,
there is sin within,
but without pride,
there is no sin.

The white man builds
a fine looking warm house
so if he dies
his family has the house for help.

Anyone who does this does right
if there is no pride.
If there is pride, there is evil,
without it all is well.

The white man keeps cattle and horses
and they are a help to his family
if he should die
his family has the stock for help.

No evil will follow
if the animals are fed well,
kindly treated
and not overworked.

Now all this is right
if there is no pride.

So they said and he said.
It was that way.

DRINKING

Some have said
there is no harm
in drinking fermented liquids.

Let this plan be followed:

let men gather in two parties,
one having a feast of food,
apples and corn
while the other party drinks
hard cider and whiskey.

Let the parties be evenly
divided and matched
and let them commence
at the same time.

When the feast is over
you will see those who drank
murder their own people.

So they said and he said.
It was that way.

THE WHITES

You have had the constant fear
the white race
will wipe you out.

The Creator will care
for his real people.

So they said and he said.
It was that way.

GREED

Now they said to him
"We will pause here
in order for you to see."

And as he watched,
he saw a large woman
sitting there.
She was grasping frantically
at all the things
within her reach
and because of her great size
she could not stand.
That was what he saw.

Then they asked him,
"What did you see?"

He answered,
"It is hard to say.
I saw a woman great of size,
snatching at all that was about her.
It seemed she could not rise."

Then the messengers answered,
"It is true.
What you saw
was the evil of greed.
She cannot stand
and will remain thus forever.

Thus it will be always with those
who think more of the things of earth
than of this new world above.
They cannot stand upon the heaven road."

So they said and he said.
It was that way.

THE HOUSE WITH A SPIRE

It was not long before they said,
"We must stop here."

Then they pointed
in a certain direction
and commanded him to watch.

As he watched he saw a house
with a spire and a path
leading into the house.
No path led out.
There was no door
and no windows in that house.

A great noise came
from within the house
of wailing and crying
and the house was hot.

Then they asked him
what he saw.

He answered,
"I saw a house with a spire
and a path leading in.
There was no door.
There were no windows.
Within was a great noise,
wailing and crying
and the house was hot."

The messengers replied,
"You have truly seen.
For an Indian to follow
the beliefs of
the whites' religion
is a hard thing."

So they said and he said.
It was that way.

MEDICINE

The messengers commanded him
to give attention and he did.
Then he saw a great assembly
and the assembly was singing,

"The whole earth is gathered here.
All the world may come to us.
We are ready."

Then the messengers said,
"What did you see?"

He answered,
"I saw a great gathering of beings
and all of them were singing
and the words they sang were,

'The whole earth is gathered here.
All the world may come to us.
We are ready.' "

Then the messengers said,
"It is very true
The beings you saw
looked like human creatures.
It is true that they are singing.

That assembly is a gathered host
of the medicines of healing.
Now let this be your ceremony
when you gather plants of medicine:

First offer tobacco.
Then tell the plant
in gentle words
what you desire of it
and pluck it from its roots.

It is said in the upper world
it is not right to take a plant
for medicine without
first talking to it.

Let none ever be taken
without first speaking."

So they said and he said.
It was that way.

THE CORN SPIRIT

The day was bright
when I went into the planted field
and alone I wandered
in the planted field
and it was the time
of the second hoeing.

A woman suddenly appeared
and threw her arms
around my neck
and as she held me
she spoke, saying,

    "When you leave this earth
    for the new world above
    it is our wish to follow you."

I looked for the woman
but saw only
the long leaves of corn
twining about my shoulders.

Then I understood
it was the Spirit of Corn
who had spoken
She, the sustainer of life.

So I replied,
"O Spirit of the Corn
do not follow me
but abide on the earth,
be strong and faithful
to your purpose.

Ever endure and do not fail
the children of women.

It is not time
for you to follow,
for the Good Message
is but in its beginning."

It was that way.

THE CREATOR AND THE EVIL-MINDED ONE

There is a dispute in the Heaven-world
about you, Children of earth.

Two beings are disputing —
the Great Ruler, our Creator
and the Evil-Minded Spirit.

You on earth
do not know the things of heaven.

The Evil One said,
"I am the ruler of the earth
because when I command
I speak but once and the people obey."

The Great Ruler answered,
"The earth is mine
for I created it
and you helped me in no way."

The Evil One said,
"I do not hear your words
but say that when I say
to human beings 'Obey Me,' they obey,
but they do not hear your voice."

The Great Ruler replied,
"Truly the children are mine
for they have never done evil."

But the Evil One said,
"No, the children are mine
for when I bid them, 'Pick up that stick
and strike your brother,'
they obey me quickly."

Then was the Great Ruler sad
and he said,
"Once more I will send for my Messengers
and tell them my heart.
They will tell my people
and I shall redeem them."

But the Evil One said,
"Even so it will not be long
before human beings again break your way.
With one word I destroy it
for they do my bidding.
I delight in the name Hanisseono
and those who love my name
will find me behind them
when they speak it
though they be
at the ends of the earth."

Then the Great Ruler
spoke to the Four Messengers saying,

"Go and tell the human beings
that they must not call me The Great Ruler,
for the Evil One calls himself
The Ruler of Mankind.
Whoever is turned into my way,
must say when he calls me, 'Our Creator,'
and whoever speaks
the Evil One's name
must say 'The Tormentor.'

Then will the Evil One know
they have discovered who he truly is,
for he is the one who will punish the wicked
when they depart from this world."

So they said and he said.
It was that way.

44

CORN PLANTING

It is a custom
to make a thanksgiving
over the hills of planted corn.

Let the head of the family
make this invocation
that the corn may continue
to support human life.

Now this will be
a right thing to do.
Whoever asks help
of the Creator
will receive it.

THE LAST SONG

Each person has
a song to sing
when their time comes
to leave the earth.

When a person departs
they must sing that song
and continue to sing
all along on their journey
to the other world.

Those who have repented
and believe the Good Message
will do this.

So they said and he said.
It was that way.

III   Not a Thing of Paint and Feathers

THE MIDDLE CANOE

It is good to live,
we sing and cannot stand.
We are afraid of no one,
we sing and cannot see.

The Horned Serpent
raises his head from the water,
beckons and we fall.

The water burns around us,
our dreams burn within.
Hot as melted pewter
is this rum we drink.

Those in the boats
on either side
are only called our guardians
because their vision
still can reach
one bank of this river
which has no end.

THE SNOW

It is the month
when snow leaves the fields.
My people return
from trading furs,
canoes awash with rum.
It leaves them colder
than that winter
when Sullivan, the Town Destroyer,
marched through our hearts
burning even the places
of those who took the Americans' part.

I watch my people
through blurred eyes.
More have died this season
from the fevers of rum
than fell on the field of Oriskany
where the British put us in the forward lines.

I close my eyes
and dream of those who died,
of a war lost in treaties
made by those we called brothers.
Papers claimed our lands.
Bottles claimed our souls.

I dream of those,
eyes open in the snow,
who lie, their limbs
turning into cold fire.

THE NIGHT

It is night outside
and night within.
My soul shakes
with the wild cries
of the raftsmen
drifting on the Allegany,
returning from Pittsburgh
where they sold the skins
of our brothers, the animals
for this same fire
which tears my own throat.

My daughter brings me water.
I ask her for rum,
though my hands
can barely hold the cup.

The moons change.
I look for my heart.
I listen for a voice to tell me
it is not caught forever
in the dark glass of bottles
which glint brighter
than the drowned eyes
of silent raftsmen.

GANIO-DAI'YO AT COLD SPRING, 1809

from the Journal of William Allinson

Blaze of vermillion paint
from the corner of each eye,
two silver quills from each ear,
one erect with a tuft of red feathers.

Nearly bald, forehead painted red,
of grave countenance.
He looked venerable.

On his arms were
silver bracelets,
his leggings of red cloth
and his covering
a blanket all over —
which he threw off in council
and took up his long pipe.

CORNPLANTER SPEAKS OF HANDSOME LAKE

He made many mistakes,
so it is reported.

He was only a man
and men
are liable to make mistakes.

What he did and said
of himself
is of no consequence.

What he did and said
by the direction
of the Four Messengers
is everything.

We do not worship him.
We worship One Great Creator.

TONAWANDA

The strings of wampum
which belonged to Handsome Lake
tell the Good Message.
No white
has ever seen them.

At Tonawanda
they may be brought out
once each two years
at the beginning
of the long circuit of preaching
the prophet's words
from Longhouse to Longhouse
which begins each fall.
He who bears the title Ganio-dai'yo
is their custodian.

Yet if even one cloud
is in the sky,
the strings may not
be brought into the open.
Whenever an anthropologist
is present at
that meeting,
there is always
one small cloud
which can be found.

NOT A THING OF PAINT OR FEATHERS

It was said by the Reverend
William Beauchamp that the way
of Handsome Lake, in his day,
was fast dying out
and that was in 1907.

And Arthur Parker,
whose father was Seneca,
told of the grief
of an Onondaga Teller of the Gai'wiio
over the passing of the old way
and that was in 1913.

And each of those who have written
of the Iroquois have clearly seen
that those old people
who knew the chants, the medicines,
the songs, the stories
have been growing fewer.

Yet the songs grow stronger
each Midwinter and those who come
to the Longhouses to hear
The Good Message
know that their belief
is not a thing of paint or feathers
but of the heart.

MIDWINTER AT ONONDAGA

Faces of basswood and pounded metal
faces of whirlwind and horse hair
faces of spirits which come to dreamers
you have returned
we bid you welcome.

The Corn Husk dancer
leads you through the door
the sounds of gunfire
you burst past guards
and with bare hands
you lift the coals
red as your faces
from the pot-bellied stoves
black as your faces
and scatter the ashes
a blessing on our shoulders.

We guess your dreams
which are always the same —
tobacco, scorched corn pudding and bread.
And the old exchange
is made again
as we give you the real tobacco,
onyengwa-onweh, which you stuff
into your many pockets
as we feed you ojiskwa,
the scorched corn pudding,
as the women gently touch your faces.

You give us health
you quiet our nights
bring us a solemn
joyous laughter, your hunched backs
bearing the weight of power
your Turtle shell rattles
echoing voices brought from caves
we must stoop to enter,
stone which lends you strength.

Defenders, Grandfathers
your healing breath grows stronger
each year as you drive out evil.
You who see where we cannot,
your children bid you welcome.

WHEN THE GOOD MIND GAMBLED

When the Good Mind,
the Creator, gambled
with his Grandmother,
mother of his mother,
Earth,
   his pieces in the game
   were living things,
   the heads of Chicakadees
     which fell in the way
     which made him the winner
   in the game that decided
     the right for life
     to continue.
And so it is
that the Longhouse People
have lived,
   each morning's new breath
     a winning cast of the dice.

ENDNOTES

P. 5 "Thanksgiving"

: GANIO-DAI'YO . . . Handsome Lake
"It is a Handsome Lake," one of the
names passed down traditionally
among the Senecas to "chiefs" who
are representatives to the Great
League of Peace.

P. 9 "I"

: STRAWBERRY MOON . . . the month
of June
THE KEEPERS OF THE WESTERN DOOR
. . . The Seneca People
The Iroquois people saw the shape
of their Great League in the form
of a *Longhouse*, the traditional Iroquois dwelling. Every longhouse
was aligned east to west, with a
door at either end; the fire was in
the center. Some of these longhouses were very large, over 300
feet long, and they were the homes
of many families, each having its
own "apartment" against one of the
two walls. If you imagine an ex-
tended longhouse superimposed
over the area that the Iroquois
League's Five Nations lived in it
looks like this:

ONEIDA

ONONDAGA (Keepers of the Fire)
Syracuse

SENECA
Keepers
of the Western Door)
Buffalo

MOHAWK
(Keepers of the
Eastern Door)
Albany

CAYUGA

P. 14 "The White Dog Feast": THE WHITE DOG FEAST . . . Like most American Indian people, the Iroquois kept dogs both as pets and for food. One of the sacred ceremonies involved the preparation and eating of a special breed of white dog.

P. 36 "Farming" : OUR YOUNGER BROTHERS . . . The white people

P. 49 "The Middle Canoe" : THE MIDDLE CANOE . . . it had become a common practice, when the fortunes of the Seneca were at their lowest ebb, for those returning on the river from trading furs to place the ones most drunk in the middle canoe to keep them from falling out without being seen and drowning.

*Typeset in 11 pt. Janson by David Martin, Types, Inc.
of Greensboro. The display pages were handset and hand-
printed by Alan Brilliant. The text was printed by Edwards
Brothers, Inc.: five hundred cloth and five hundred paper.*

The Unicorn Keepsake Series
is edited by Teo Savory.

6091